For Nikolaus's grandchildren, Wes and Veda

BOXER BOOKS Ltd. and the distinctive Boxer Books logo
are trademarks of Union Square & Co., LLC.

Union Square & Co., LLC, is a subsidiary of Sterling Publishing Co., Inc.

© 2024 Alexandra Milton

All rights reserved. No part of this publication may be reproduced, stored in a retrieval system, or transmitted in any form or by any means (including electronic, mechanical, photocopying, recording, or otherwise) without prior written permission from the publisher.

This edition first published in the United States and Canada in 2024 by Boxer Books Limited.

ISBN 978-1-915801-86-9

Library of Congress Control Number: 2023949809

For information about custom editions, special sales, and premium purchases,
please contact specialsales@unionsquareandco.com.

Printed in China

Lot #:

2 4 6 8 10 9 7 5 3 1

05/24

unionsquareandco.com

Who Lives Here?

Alexandra Milton

Boxer Books

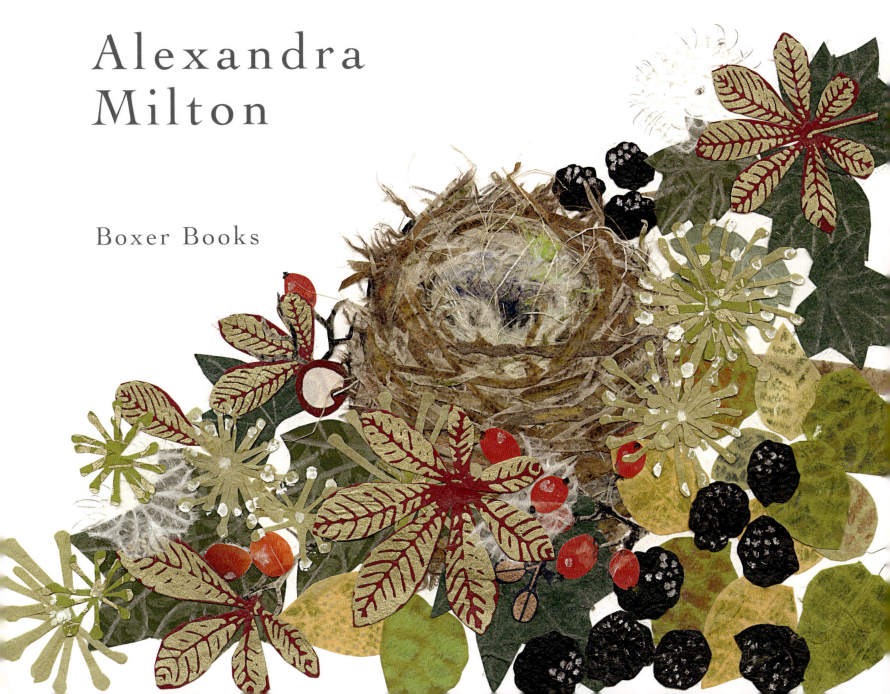

Look, in the field,
there's a bundle of grass.
Let's get closer.
What can we see?

Who lives here?
Who can it be?

A small harvest mouse!

Harvest mice shelter in tiny ball-shaped nests woven from grass. They build slightly bigger nests—the size of a tennis ball—for raising their young.

Here, in the hedge,
there's a small nest of twigs.
Let's get nearer.
What can we see?

Who lives here?
Who can it be?

A plump little wren!

Male wrens build several simple nests. Female wrens bond with the male who has built the most nests, then decide which is the best one before padding it out and laying their eggs.

Down by those roots,
there's a deep, dark hole.
Let's peer inside.
What can we see?

Who lives here?
Who can it be?

A long-eared rabbit!

Rabbits dig underground burrows in which they live with their extended family. Lots of different burrows are connected to each other by a network of tunnels called a warren.

Next to the water,
there's a stack of wet sticks.
Don't go too close!
What can we see?

Who lives here?
Who can it be?

A big-toothed beaver!

A beaver's home is called a lodge. Most of its entrances are underwater. Some are extra wide for bringing in large items of food.

Watch where you step,
there's some freshly dug earth.
Let's walk around it.
What can we see?

Who lives here?
Who can it be?

A black velvety mole!

Moles spend most of their life in underground tunnels. They dig separate rooms for sleeping, raising their young, and storing food. The soil they dig out forms little molehills on the surface.

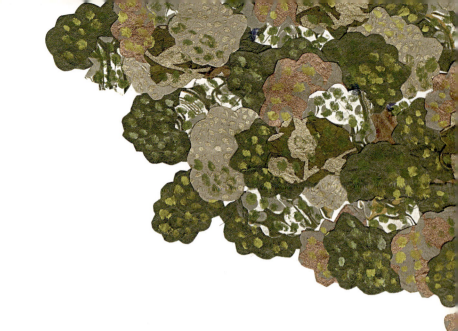

A great big tree, all branches and leaves,
and two round eyes that are staring at me.
Let's get closer. What can we see?
Who lives here? Who can it be?

A sharp-eyed owl lives in this tree.

Many owls make their nests in the hollows of trees. They don't make the hole themselves, but use holes left behind by other animals. Once they find a place they like, they often use it for the rest of their lives.